YOU ARE HERE
Departed
Arrived
21¢
Belvidere
R353 BELVIDERE
78
DESTINATION: SOMEWHERE
ANY ROUTE PERMITTED
VALID FOR TRAVEL

D0548778

To: THE DODDS

From: RUDGE

For the love of travel and adventure

Copyright © 2016 by Leila Rudge

All rights reserved. No part of this book may be reproduced, transmitted, or stored in an information retrieval system in any form or by any means, graphic, electronic, or mechanical, including photocopying, taping, and recording, without prior written permission from the publisher.

First U.S. edition 2016

Library of Congress Catalog Card Number 2015909438
ISBN 978-0-7636-8954-4

CCP 21 20 19 18 17 16
10 9 8 7 6 5 4 3 2 1

Printed in Shenzhen, Guangdong, China

This book was typeset in Mrs. Eaves.
The illustrations were done in mixed media.

Candlewick Press
99 Dover Street
Somerville, Massachusetts 02144

visit us at www.candlewick.com

Admit One

Gary

LEILA RUDGE

CANDLEWICK PRESS

WITHDRAWN

BY AIR MAIL
Poule D
19

Most of the time,
Gary was just like
the other racing pigeons.

He ate the same seeds.
Slept in the same loft.
And dreamed of adventure.

But on race days, when the pigeons set off in the travel basket, Gary stayed at home.

To pass the time, he organized his scrapbook.

He had a collection of travel mementos from everywhere.

Except Gary had never been anywhere.
Because Gary couldn't fly.

5/10
22:30
0
12

The racing pigeons usually returned just before supper.

And they always discussed wind directions and flight paths. Or waypoints.

Gary loved hearing about their adventures.

He would perch nearby and record everything in his scrapbook.

But one night, Gary leaned too far on his perch.
And lost his balance.

Gary and his scrapbook fell down
to the bottom of the loft.

And they both
landed in the
travel basket
with a bump.

The next day was race day, and Gary traveled
a very long way from home.

By the time Gary woke up, the sky was full of feathers and flapping wings.

The racing pigeons were racing!

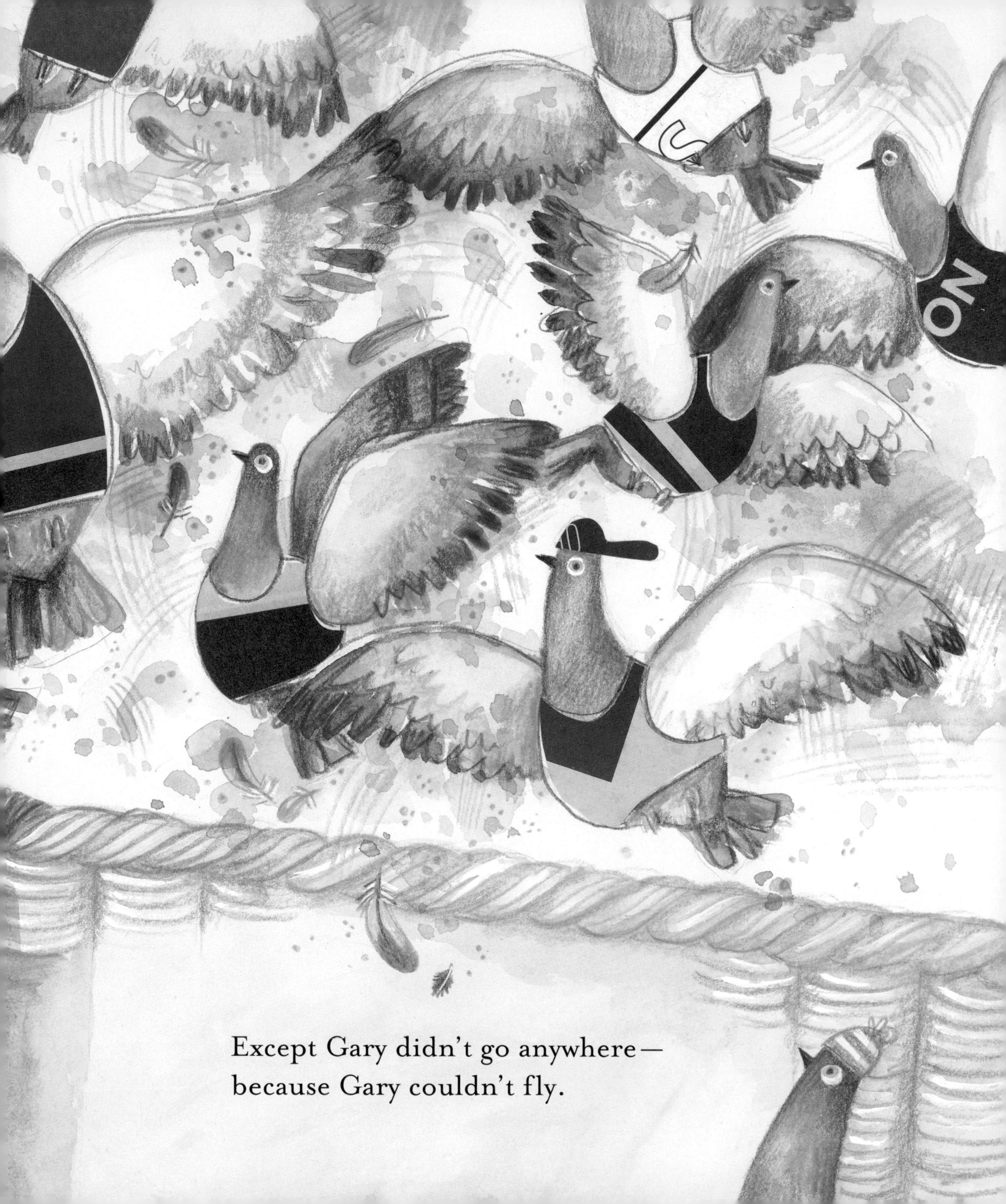

Except Gary didn't go anywhere—
because Gary couldn't fly.

Soon the other pigeons
were dots in the distance.

They were flying back
to the loft.

Gary wondered if
he would ever
find a way home.

Or if he would be lost in the city forever.

P
RAILROAD CROSSING
ALL DIRECTIONS
STRAIGHT AHEAD
LEFT
RIGHT
RIGHT TURN ONLY
FOLLOW

Gary's collection of travel mementos always perked him up. So he opened up his scrapbook.

Gradually, the city came to feel a little more familiar.

And Gary felt a little less lost.

(Ticket is valid for travel on any route from here to there or anywhere.)
MODE OF TRANSPORT:
Direction of travel:
HOME
Route B
Admit one
BRIDGE CROSSING

Before long, Gary had plotted
his own way back to the loft.

50

Gary arrived home just before supper.
He had all sorts of new travel mementos
for his scrapbook.

And the most adventurous adventure story.
Gary couldn't fly. But Gary had been everywhere!

Most of the time, Gary is just
like the other racing pigeons.

He eats the same seeds.
Sleeps in the same loft.
And dreams of adventure.

But on some days . . .

3
en vue de
mettre à u
au t
- des PRES
en NY
- de L'INV
- de L'INAP
- des CURE

the other pigeons are just like Gary.

31901060090687